The Animals' Ball

The
Animals' Ball

by Hélène Tersac

paintings by Frédéric Clément

A Star & Elephant Book

The Green Tiger Press

1983

The door closed softly. In bed, waiting, Eloise listened to her mother's footsteps fading away down the stairs into silence. A pause. A few more footsteps — imagined or actually heard? Then silence.

The crack of light beneath the door had disappeared. The landing was dark. Even though her mind was made up, she still had to wait; neither stir, nor fall asleep. And wait still more. Now it might well be nine o'clock. Perhaps ten.

To pass the time Eloise began to examine all the objects in her room, one by one. But she couldn't concentrate on any one of them for as long as she had promised herself. Her scrutiny of the room was quickly over. Tonight there was not even a single gnat flitting around her bedside lamp to divert her. Eloise found her gaze fixed upon the wallpaper, where, close beside her, tiny intricate patterns seemed to move in ever growing arabesques, never ceasing, which carried her thoughts far away . . .

She began counting, reached 8,999, and stopped. She lacked the heart to begin all over again, and almost got out of bed. She remembered herself just in time. She must wait. But the wait seemed never-ending! She stared at the ceiling. It was white.

She turned in her bed and turned again. Once again she settled her doll into place beside her. Once again she stared at the ceiling. She adjusted herself so that she was almost sitting up, took her doll in her arms, bent down to her and whispered, "Wait a little bit longer — we'll get there." At that moment, she heard the music.

At last!

*E*loise rose from her bed, slipped into her dressing gown, and, holding her doll by the hand, she went to the door, opened it, and stole out onto the landing. Without a sound, she closed the door behind her.

It was dark.

Creeping along the landing on tip-toe, she reached the stairs and started down them making herself very small. Every three or four steps, she would stop, standing up to peer over the banister. No, she couldn't really see well enough. She still had to go down a few steps further.

Eloise was torn between the temptation to go further so she could see better, and her fear of being caught. Just a few steps more.

She reached the second landing and crossed it with a pounding heart, forcing herself to go on to the next step and then one step more. There she sat down and did not move. From this step, her forehead pressing against the bars of the banister, she was able to see everything.

*V*oices and music floated up to her. As she leaned forward, staring, she saw shadows and movements that seemed to belong to no one, shadows that passed by and moved on again. Sometimes a figure, a hand holding a glass, a laugh, made her think vaguely, but very fleetingly, that all this had nothing to do with the people she knew — with anyone human. It was difficult to tell — the room was aswirl with gowns, furs, fabrics, with twilight shadows and music. But there were few faces. Eloise leaned forward a little further to see more clearly.

Not a single face.

*H*alf-glimpsed figures, cascading ruffles, movement. A suffused light. Here and there a candlestick. A piano. A black cat — Licorice, the house cat. What was *he* doing there?

Eloise was reassured when she saw her mother gliding past. She tried to follow her with her eyes and even craned her head up a bit, at the risk of being seen, but quickly her mother's silhouette disappeared. And there, in her place, she saw only a fox.

She thought she saw a fox. A fox who didn't run away. Quite to the contrary — a fox who stood and chatted with great assurance. With her mother. Then he began to dance, alone, upright, paws held to the front.

The fox drifted away, as mysteriously as he appeared. "A fox?"

he music became softer and the lights brightened. Eloise settled comfortably into her perch on the stairs and curled up. Then she sat up again. Plates appeared and hands reached out for glasses that passed, sparkling from one hand to another. A lion drank the contents of the glass handed to him, set it down on the tray, and withdrew rapidly on all fours. Eloise had only enough time to see his tail disappearing into the bushes outside, where, on the topmost branch, a squirrel was perched, busily shelling a nut.

*A*ll the French windows against the garden must have been opened. Eloise could not see them from where she sat, but she guessed as much because, little by little, the large ballroom emptied in that direction.

Only the wolf remained behind, standing very tall, all alone by the bar. He had human hands, and on one of them was a gold ring which looked just like her uncle's. But her uncle was not a wolf, and wolves don't wear rings . . .

A princess entered. Walking with stately steps, she advanced toward the wolf, stopped beside him, and bent close. They began to talk, but Eloise couldn't hear what they were saying, even when she cupped her hand to her ear. Were they speaking in the language of wolves or the language of princesses? Taking the princess by the hand, the wolf led her from the bar, and they began to dance. Was he a wolf from the forest?

The wolf danced very well, with real grace, inclining his muzzle toward the face of the princess, likely murmuring a few words to her from time to time.

*T*he music stopped. The princess and the wolf parted. Then a thousand people entered, and with them a thousand animals, so that Eloise could not distinguish those who wore cloth from those who wore fur. It was chilly, and the women were doubtless keeping their furs on, like the animals.

Where, now, was the wolf?

Eloise was sure she recognized the back of her father's neck with its birthmark that had always intrigued her. So the musketeer talking with the donkey must be her father! But the donkey had curious hooves, different for the front feet than for those behind. In fact, his hind feet seemed to be clad in shoes. But in these shadows, how could she be sure?

Suddenly the donkey gave forth a resounding "hee-haw" and her father burst into laughter. There was more laughter. Then, quickly, other animal cries joined in. Were these the cries of animals from the forest? Then still more laughter and the clinking of glasses.

*T*he music began again — it was a waltz. Eloise smiled. Her mother danced on. But, with the wolf?

Eloise held tightly to the banister. From the deep night of the garden she heard rustling and the sound of branches creaking. But she could see nothing, nothing at all.

When the waltz had ended, Eloise was relieved to see the wolf take his leave, after making a little bow, that she thought very awkward. Then she turned her attention to her mother, determined not to lose sight of her this time. Watching her move farther away, she longed to call out "Mama," but she restrained herself.

The wolf had completely disappeared. So had her mother.

The dancing began again. But the dancers' feet were so close together, the fabric of their garments so intermingled, that it was impossible to guess whose bodies were under the fabrics; impossible to recognize whose faces were under the makeup and the masks. All were hidden. Would she know them?

From where did the countesses and princesses come? Who were they? Had they come from the forest? In lace and in velvet, elegant coiffures and ringlets, hats and wigs. Whom did the elaborate costumes hide? Animals who spoke, laughed, danced. Who were they?

Eloise no longer felt cold. Neither did she feel drowsy. She watched and waited. Now and then a gloved hand was ungloved, allowing her to glimpse a hand that she recognized, or thought she recognized, a hand that perhaps she would recognize before the wolf came back.

The fox entered once more — he was small, but large for a fox, and he continued to stand upright on his hind paws. He was bold, not always trying to hide himself like other foxes. He even strode up to the foot of the stairs and leaned against the banister, gazing up towards her. But the stairway was shadowy and the fox didn't see Eloise. She told herself that she had been right not to venture any further down the stairs . . .

This fox didn't look like a real fox, not at all. He wasn't like the wolf, either. Would he come back?

And where was her father? Was he dancing in the garden? Was he with her mother? With another countess? Or was he playing with the animals, as he knew how to do so well?

There were many comings and goings from the salon to the garden, and from the garden to the salon, lights that blazed and lights that dimmed, an immense cake all lit up which crossed the room, the sounds of clapping and of a melody that Eloise remembered hearing at her birthday celebration.

*E*loise closed her eyes, took a few steps into the garden, and began walking toward the forest.

The further she went from the house, the thicker the silence and the darkness became. She tried not to be frightened thinking as hard as she could of other little girls who had crossed the forest all alone in the night without being eaten by a wolf. After all, *"There aren't any wolves in the forest anymore."* But the snapping of twigs under her feet, and the branches catching at her hair, even when she didn't leave the path, were very unsettling all the same.

The moon, though it was often hidden by the clouds, gave her a little light that kept her from straying off the path. But as the moon shone upon the path, it also shed light on thick woods to the left and right, and on the tree tops, and on the whole of the forest. And that light, too, was disturbing.

*E*loise was now in the middle of the forest. She turned half around and fear seized her as she stopped. But again she decided to go forward in order to get at least to the Crossways of the Fourteen Brothers. The owl was always in this area, hidden at the top of an old ruined mansion.

It was too late to go back. Eloise heard the owl, shuddered, saw him, and began to run to get as far away as possible. She slowed down a little, then walked with long strides, and then again began to run. Surely the wolf was in these thickets. It was necessary to get home as quickly as possible. Or else!

When Eloise opened her eyes again, she was sitting on the edge of the stairs. She leaned over; down below the light was blazing; she listened to the music, and in the midst of the commotion she heard the small sounds of kisses. She stared at people and animals pressed together, she saw enormous paws resting on bare shoulders, animal manes mingling with the coils of ladies' hair, muzzles so long that faces had to keep their distances for a kiss on a cheek, so as not to be gobbled up altogether. She heard laughter and still more kisses.

Then a brief moment of silence.

Finally — doors opening at the front of the house, footsteps on the walkway, the engines of cars. A few more sentences drifting up to her from far off.

loise scarcely heard the sound of footsteps mounting the stairs. She felt herself being lifted into someone's arms, and when she felt herself hugged close and was sure they were the arms of her mother, she opened her eyes to see her mother's smile.

"Couldn't you sleep?" Eloise shook her head slightly.

"Then you saw the ball and all the costumes?" And, as her mother was still smiling and hugging her, Eloise said "Yes" very softly.

Tucked into her bed, her mother sitting beside her, Eloise caught a glimpse of her father softly approaching her bedside, his face questioning. She heard her mother say, "Hush, she's asleep." Eloise's mother put her finger to her lips.

The text, set in Clearface Roman, was done by Thompson Type of San Diego, California.
Color separations by Color Graphics of San Diego, California.
Binding by Hiller Industries, Salt Lake City, Utah.
Designed by Sandra Darling & Judythe Sieck.
Printed at the Green Tiger Press,
La Jolla, California.